Pirates in the Yard

by

Hugh Kingsley

Published by The Brainary®

Dedicated

to

Jonathan, Samuel, and Lisa.

Special thanks

to

Dr Lawrence Shapiro, Karen Schader &

Dr Franklin Rubenstein for their wonderful

guidance and encouragement.

Cerebellum Islands

Desert

Bay of Plenty

N
O
E
S

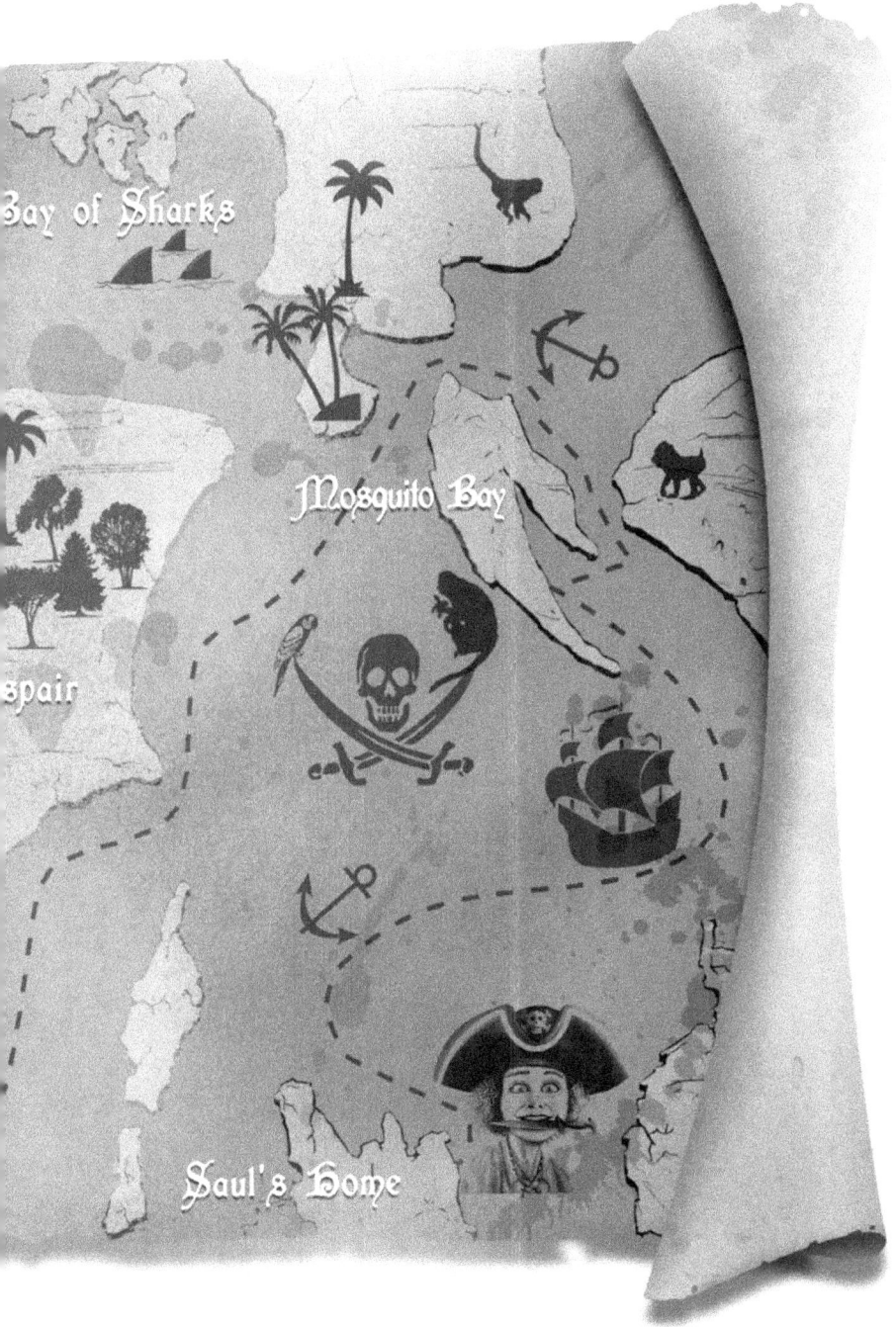

Bay of Sharks

Mosquito Bay

spair

Saul's Home

Published by The Brainary® Australia and The Brainary® LLC United States of America
Registered Office: 45 Pakington Street Geelong West 3218 Victoria Australia
Registered Office: 325 Post Road West Westport CT 06880 United States of America
www.thebrainary.com Hugh@thebrainary.com
First published by The Brainary® September 20, 2012

ISBN: 978-0-9873476-0-2 (pbk)
ISBN: 978-0-9873476-1-9 (e-Book)

Title copyright: Pirates in the Yard© 2012
Text copyright: Hugh Kingsley© 2012
Illustrations: Alberto Verdejo 2012 http://sikkilustrisegno.blogspot.com/

British Library Cataloguing in Publication Data
Kingsley, Hugh
Pirates in the yard
1. Adventure stories 2. Children's stories.
I. Title
823.9'2-dc23
ISBN-13: 9780987347602

National Library of Australia Cataloguing-in-Publication entry
Author: Kingsley, Hugh.
Title: Pirates in the yard / Hugh Kingsley.

ISBN: 9780987347602 (pbk.)
Target Audience: For primary school age.

Subjects: Pirates—Juvenile fiction.
Adventure stories

Dewey Number: A823.4

Contents

Chapter One: As If!

 As Saul stood at the kitchen window drinking a glass of water, he was amazed to find a fully rigged pirate ship sailing along his street. The skinny sixth-grader rubbed his eyes and thought, "I'm daydreaming!" His mind raced as it tried to make sense of what he was seeing.

He looked through the window once more. To his amazement, the pirate ship was still there. In fact, this time it was even larger and closer. "I'm sleepwalking. No, I know. It's a mirage!" thought Saul. He peered suspiciously at the water. Was there something funny in it?

He splashed cold water over his face, dampening his wavy blond hair. Now he was sure he was wide-awake and in full control of his senses. For the third time, Saul looked through the window. "It's real, it's real," he muttered excitedly.

The huge wooden ship had three masts, each with its own lookout. At its stern, a bright red and black pirate flag complete with skull and crossbones fluttered in the breeze, and an impressive bronze dog's head adorned its bow. Dressed in a resplendent uniform, the captain stood tall and erect next to the helmsman, who gripped the wheel.

His heart and mind racing, his muscles tensed like a lion ready to spring into action—pow!—Saul ran at full speed to the front of his house where his mom and dad lay fast asleep.

"Mom, dad, wake up!" Saul yelled. "There's a ... there's a pirate ship ... and it's ..." But no matter how hard he tried, Saul could not get the words out of his mouth clearly. His yelling startled his mother, who instantly woke up thinking something was wrong. Even his dad stopped snoring and, struggling upright, foggily asked, "Are you okay?"

"There's a pirate ship ... and it's—" repeated Saul.

His dad interrupted with a snort and said, "You're dreaming, Saul. Go back to bed. It's too early to get up now."

His mom nodded her agreement. "Saul. Go back to bed and read a book."

Saul was excited, frustrated, and exasperated—all at the same time. Why wouldn't his parents take him seriously? If only he had been able to get his words out coherently ... But excitement and curiosity quickly took over, and Saul raced back to the kitchen. Still in his PJs, he watched from the open back door. Several pirates were lowering the sails, while the helmsman steered the ship toward the side gates of his house.

"Ahoy there, ahoy there, open the gates or we'll attack!" the captain ordered.

Momentarily, Saul froze with fear. Then he picked up on the captain's mischievous yet friendly tone, which reminded him of his dad. He decided that the captain would be just like dad, all mischief and fun, but no serious threat.

Springing into action, Saul exchanged his PJs for shorts and a T-shirt, grabbed his flip-flops, and raced out the back door. As the screen door banged behind him, he opened the gates and yelled out to the captain, "Welcome ashore, Captain!" He could hardly believe that he was standing confidently in front of a huge pirate ship, inviting it into his backyard.

The image of his parents asleep in bed popped into his mind, and after excusing himself, Saul zoomed back into the house. The screen door banged loudly behind him as he flew down the corridor to his parents' bedroom once more.

This time, Saul got his words out clearly and convincingly. Naturally, dad remained fast asleep, snoring and snorting, but mom hurried out of bed, and dressed in a T-shirt and skirt. After slipping on her flip-flops, she joined Saul in the kitchen.

Like Saul, mom thought she was dreaming at first. And like Saul, she rubbed her eyes and splashed some cold water over her face. But the pirate ship did not go away. In fact, it grew larger in size and closer to the back door.

"See, it's true; it's true!" exclaimed Saul. "Please, mom, can we invite the pirates inside?"

"No," said his mom in a suspicious and serious voice. "They are pirates, and pirates have a terrible reputation for plundering and murdering people."

"Please, mom, please," Saul repeated. "Maybe these are friendly pirates, but we won't know unless we invite them in. Besides, dad will come to our rescue if I'm wrong."

"What use would dad be?" Mom thought. "He's fast asleep and thinks this is all a dream."

Saul's contagious enthusiasm soon got the better of his mom. "Just this once," she said—just the way many moms do in special situations like this one.

Later, Saul would learn that the pirates were being chased by Captain Hammerhead of the *Black Drag-*

on. Captain Hammerhead was known to be a powerful and cruel pirate feared by all who came within his reach. But for now, Saul and his mom welcomed the ship with a wave.

Chapter Two: No Saul

 After the pirates tied their ship to the back of Saul's house, the captain and his mate came ashore and into the kitchen. A colorful parrot perched on the captain's left shoulder; a small brown monkey trailed behind. The captain, who was tall, slender, and well tanned, looked handsome and powerful in his smart uniform. He wore black knee-high boots, crimson velvet breeches, and a matching waistcoat over a white silk shirt. A red silk sash was tied around his waist, and a black leather sash crossed his waistcoat diagonally. A hat adorned with brightly colored feathers of purple, deep blue, crimson, and violet sat squarely on his wavy blond hair.

His mate looked impressive, but he was no match for the captain in style: no knee-high leather boots or crimson waistcoat or leather sash. Rather, he had on black leather shoes with a gold buckle (which he wore only when on land) and a three-cornered hat. He was dressed for action, not appearance.

Surprisingly, the two men were very friendly and polite (although somewhat smelly). The captain spoke first. "I am Captain Bartholomew Maverick of the Golden Retriever at your service. This is Quartermaster Hawkeye, and these rascals are Popeye and Diego." Simultaneously, Captain Maverick and Quartermaster Hawkeye removed their pirate hats and bowed.

Mom was most impressed and responded with her best manners. "My name is Lisa and this is my son, Saul. Please take a seat at our kitchen table." Having said so, she immediately felt worried. "What business do these pirates really have with our family?" she thought.

It was as if Captain Maverick had read her mind. "We are friendly pirates on an adventure," he said. "We do not wish to plunder or murder anyone in your house. We come in peace and are in need of fresh water and supplies before continuing on our adventure."

Mom was intrigued. "Please join us for breakfast?" she offered.

"Yes, thank you," responded Captain Maverick graciously.

Mom made them bacon and eggs with toast, an she even gave them some of dad's favorite homemade strawberry jam.

"Yum," thought Hawkeye.

Saul, knowing a bit about pirates, asked, "Would you like to wash your breakfast down with some rum?"

Before Captain Maverick or Hawkeye could answer, mom blurted out, "Not on your life, Saul! I am *not* going to serve these pirates any rum in my house." She turned to the two pirates and said, "Captain Maverick and Quartermaster Hawkeye, would you like some tea or coffee?"

The parrot, Popeye, squawked, "No rum Maverick, no rum Maverick," while the monkey, Diego, satisfied himself rummaging around the kitchen floor looking for scraps of food to eat.

Sensing mom's concern, Captain Maverick was quick to accept her generous offer of tea or coffee and changed the subject. He told mom and Saul fabulous stories of their pirate adventures while sailing the seven seas, of places they had seen and lessons they had learned. As he spoke, Popeye squawked comments here and there.

Saul got to hold Hawkeye's cutlass and dagger. Hawkeye even let Saul wear his pirate hat, smelly as it was. "Can I hold your pistol?" asked Saul.

"No," said Hawkeye. "You might kill the wrong person. One day I might teach you how to fire it safely."

The quartermaster was somewhat shorter than Captain Maverick, but just as well tanned. He had straight black shoulder-length hair, huge muscles, a lean body, and the eyes of a hawk. Not much happened without his seeing it or knowing about it.

By now, both mom and Saul were mesmerized by Captain Maverick's stories. It was if nothing else existed or mattered. Without warning, the captain said, "Would you and Saul like to join me on my adventure?" Mom's and Saul's eyes lit up with excitement and enthusiasm.

Saul could tell that his mom was about to say yes, when suddenly she got all practical. Instead she said, "Captain Maverick, we cannot accept your generous invitation. Saul must attend school. He has homework and chores to do." It was true that Saul had a busy school life, which also included basketball, swimming, surfing, snowboarding, skate boarding—and boring old household chores.

Captain Maverick continued as if he had not heard her reply. "We are sailing to the Cerebellum Islands, which are located at the farthest part of the seven seas. Legend has it that hidden in the Cerebellum Islands is a cave where the source of the Power of the Cranium can be found."

"Wow," thought mom, although in truth she had no idea what power a cranium might have.

Saul begged and begged his mom, promising any-thing and everything if she changed her mind. "Please, mom; please, mom; please, mom," he kept saying in an excited voice.

And mom kept saying, "No, no, no, Saul." Then she added a few more no's, as moms often do in these situations. The more she said no, the more Saul pleaded and begged—as kids often do in these situations.

Saul's willpower was strong, and he used the same argument that had gotten mom to allow the pirates into their house. Again, mom thought, "What use would dad be?"

But after many, many no's, a "Yes, maybe" slipped out of mom's mouth. Was it a slip of her tongue, or was Saul's argument having an effect? Saul knew he was getting close, and all he needed was for his mom to say yes, without the maybe. With great de-termination, he turned to face her so that their eyes locked and in his most charming of charming voices said, "Mom, I love you. You are the best." And it was those words that did the trick.

Mom's eyes fluttered. She turned to Captain Maver-ick and asked, "How do you know these islands ex-ist? How do you know that the source of the Power of the Cranium can be found there? And anyway, what *is* the Power of the Cranium?"

Swiftly, Captain Maverick slid his left hand into his right breast pocket and withdrew an old brown leather map showing the navigational directions to the Cerebellum Islands. Then he showed mom the key to the cave that hung around his neck together with the rest of his neck jewelry.

"Wow," said an awestruck mom.

Captain Maverick went on to explain how the prophet Atlanticus had given him the map and the key with strict instructions: "Maverick, go to the Cerebellum Islands, visit the cave, find the source of the Power of the Cranium, and bring it to me."

Atlanticus was a wise old prophet who lived in a log cabin high in the hills overlooking Mosquito Bay. He had a long white beard, round spectacles, and a portly shape, which was mostly due to his love of rum. Captain Maverick had met Atlanticus many years ago when his ship was becalmed in Mosquito Bay. The bay got its name because on calm, wind-less days it became the home to bloodthirsty mos-quitoes.

Atlanticus had rescued the *Golden Retriever* from the mosquitoes by towing it ashore. He and the captain became good friends and soon shared many special times together. They would often discuss big questions like: "Is the world flat?" "Is there an underside to the earth?" "Why do mermaids look like women but have tails instead of legs?" "Is the Loch Ness monster real?" "What language do sea serpents speak?" "How did Atlantis become an underwater city?" And on and on they would talk for hours ….

The prophet became a sort of father figure to Captain Maverick, whose father had died at sea during a massive storm when the captain was just a little boy. At times, Atlanticus addressed Captain Maverick as "My son," and when he did so, the captain felt a warm glow inside his body. When Captain Maverick needed to discuss troubling issues, he would visit Atlanticus, who was a good listener and full of excellent advice. Recently, Atlanticus had decided it was time to trust "My son," Captain Maverick, with his most special secret mission: acquiring the source of the Power of the Cranium.

Not surprisingly, Captain Maverick had asked Atlanticus the same questions as mom just asked him. The prophet often answered seemingly straightforward questions with stories, anecdotes, and fairy tales. He wanted people to think about his answers, and this time was no exception.

Atlanticus began his response by saying, "The Power of the Cranium can be partly understood through this African proverb thus:

-Every morning in Africa, a gazelle wakes up.

-It knows it must run faster than the fastest lion or it will be killed.

-Every morning a lion wakes up.

-It knows it must outrun the slowest gazelle or it will starve to death.

-It does not matter whether you are a lion or a gazelle.

-When the sun comes up, you better start running."

"So it's about survival," said mom, after hearing this explanation.

"Apparently, and also competitive edge, innovativeness, imagination, and a lot more," said Captain Maverick. "According to Atlanticus, it is rumored that the first pirate to discover the Power of the Cranium will become the most powerful pirate of all time. Sharing this power could radically change the lives of every person in the world for the better. That's why Atlanticus wants it. Should it get into the wrong hands, who knows what catastrophes could result."

With that, mom changed her mind and graciously accepted Captain Maverick's invitation. But she did not know that Captain Hammerhead of the *Black Dragon* saw his ship as the fastest lion and Captain Maverick's ship as the slowest gazelle and would soon stalk them all the way to the Cerebellum Islands.

Captain Hammerhead knew that Captain Maverick had the map to the Cerebellum Islands and wanted the treasure for himself (although he was not quite sure what it was and what he could do with it). And it was best that mom did not know or she would never have allowed Saul and herself to go on the adventure.

While Captain Maverick told mom what to pack, Hawkeye took Diego and Popeye back to the *Golden Retriever* and ordered his crew to load fresh water and general supplies from Saul's house. Mom even let the pirates help themselves to her homegrown vegetable patch and her pet chickens. But when it came to Bessie, the house cow, she said, "No way!"

Meanwhile, Saul raced back to his parents' bedroom. This time he shook his dad until he stopped snoring and sat bolt upright. "Dad, dad, dad," he blurted out, "Captain Maverick, Popeye, Diego, and Quartermaster Hawkeye were in our kitchen and had breakfast with mom and me. And guess what? Captain Maverick invited us to come with him to the Cerebellum Islands. Can we go? Mom already said yes. Will you come too, dad?"

Again, dad snorted, rubbed his eyes, and said, "Saul,

do you have any idea how early it is? Please go back to bed and let me sleep." And with those words, dad returned his head to his pillow, rolled over, and started to snore again. Before completely falling back to sleep, he thought, "What am I going to do with that boy? He has such a wonderful imagination and a contagious enthusiasm for life. But why does he have to share it with me so early in the morning?"

Saul felt disappointed and sad—disappointed because his dad did not believe him and sad because he would not be coming on the adventure. However, the thought of the adventure soon overcame his feelings. He raced back to the kitchen to help his mom pack food.

By now, mom had emptied the pantry of all the food she could spare for the trip. Naturally, she wanted to leave some for dad.

Saul said, "Mom, remember to pack some rum for the pirates."

"No way!" she replied. "I'm not getting aboard any pirate ship with men who drink rum."

"Little does she know, and it's best that way," thought Saul. He decided to let go of this one and focus on the exciting adventure that was about to begin.

Chapter Three: Cast Off

 After opening the gates and un-tying the *Golden Retriever* from the back of Saul's house, the pirates raised the sails and headed her out through the gates. You'd think this would be near impossible, but Saul's backyard was unusually large, and Hawkeye was a highly skilled helmsman.

As they sailed down the side street toward the wide blue sea ahead, Saul waved good-bye to his neighbors and friends, who just stood there looking like stunned mullets. Just as Saul and his mom had, they thought they were seeing things! But before they had time to splash water over their faces, Saul and the pirate ship had passed them by.

Captain Maverick promptly set course for the Cerebellum Islands. After the sails were hoisted and full of wind, he called mom and Saul to his quarters below deck, where he gave them pirate names. Mom became known as Mrs. Morgan, and Saul became known as Master Why. Why? Because Saul never stopped asking questions. It wasn't long before Popeye added the names *Morgan* and *Why* to his repertoire.

When Hawkeye and Cook joined the group below deck, the captain instructed Cook, "Show Mrs. Morgan and Master Why to their quarters."

In their quarters, Cook gave them pirate clothes and said, "You're pirates now, so put your pirate clothes on." Master Why replaced his shorts, T-shirt, and flip-flops with green breeches, a white puffed-sleeve linen shirt, a light-green waist sash, a jeweled necklace, a bandanna, and a three-cornered hat. Like Hawkeye, his feet were bare; he kept his black gold-buckled shoes aside for the land.

Mrs. Morgan had the choice of replacing her outfit for a long, flowing dress or black breeches. Being more of a practical type, she chose the breeches, along with brown leather shoes with gold buckles, black socks, a shirt just like Master Why's, a red waistcoat, and a bandanna to match. She was not much for hats except for sun protection when working in the garden. Unlike Master Why, she chose to wear her shoes. Captain Maverick even saw to it that she would have a variety of jewelry to wear while on board.

Mrs. Morgan was almost as tall as Captain Maverick. She was pretty and pretty bright, fast on her feet and fast with her mind. And most times, way too fast with her mouth. But that's another story.

Dressed in their new clothes, both Mrs. Morgan and Master Why looked like genuine pirates. The images of twenty-first-century life soon faded into their subconscious as they adjusted to pirate life out at sea. "Awesome," said Master Why when he was told he would be sleeping in a hammock. "Oh no," said Mrs. Morgan when she was given the same news. She did not share Master Why's enthusiasm for these sleeping arrangements and, in the excitement of accepting the invitation, had not considered such matters.

Master Why was quick to develop his sea legs, but Mrs. Morgan experienced a good dose of seasickness before getting hers. Between bouts of nausea and vomiting, she wished she had packed her seasickness tablets.

Master Why spent considerable time with Hawkeye on the upper deck, where he learned about navigation and the sailing terms pirates use. True to form, Master Why asked Hawkeye question after question. "Why is the *Golden Retriever* called the *Golden Retriever*? Why does she have two decks and three masts? Why so many cannons? Is the bronze head on the bow a golden retriever?"

Meanwhile, Mrs. Morgan wandered all over the

ship acquainting herself with what was there and making mental notes of what she thought should be there but was not. Diego followed her around and developed a habit of springing out from nowhere and anywhere when Mrs. Morgan least expected it. She could regularly be heard screeching, "Oh! Diego, you are a naughty monkey. You'll be the death of me."

Diego *was* a naughty monkey and loved playing games such as hide-and-seek. You might say Mrs. Morgan was a little nosy at times, looking into things that may not have been her business. So when Diego startled her with a "Boo!" she sort of shot through the roof twice: once in surprise and the second time because she thought she had been caught prying.

While strolling along the upper deck, Mrs. Morgan would often say to the pirates, "Put sunscreen on your faces and arms, and stop looking at me in funny ways." Naturally, the pirates thought Mrs. Morgan was mad. They had never heard of sunscreen—or ultraviolet rays for that matter. She even told the pirates, "You are dirty and unfit. Go wash your clothes, brush your teeth, and wear deodorant." Fortunately for her, she said nothing about their long hair and scruffy beards!

When Mrs. Morgan tried to organize an early morning exercise program on the upper deck, the pirates decided enough was enough. They rallied behind Toothless, their aptly named spokesman, who complained to Hawkeye. "Hawkeye, no strange madwoman is going to order us around or tell us what to do on our pirate ship."

In a sympathetic voice, Hawkeye replied, "I hear you lads, and I'll take it up with the captain."

Captain Maverick's way of addressing the grievance was to host a welcoming feast so that the pirates, Mrs. Morgan, and Master Why could get to know each other better in a more relaxed atmosphere. The order went out via Hawkeye: "Prepare ye all for a feast."

In true pirate style, there was salted meat, salted fish, pickled vegetables, hard-boiled eggs, cheese, hard stick with molasses, mangoes, and grapes, and more. The pirates washed down their meal with loads of rum, and between courses could be heard hooting with laughter and singing sea chanteys. Popeye perched himself on Captain Maverick's shoulder and squawked, "Rum Maverick, rum Maverick." Diego satisfied himself with eating the scraps of food left behind by the pirates. When all had finished eating, the crew spun myths, legends, and stories about pirate life both at sea and on the land.

Believe it or not, even Mrs. Morgan had some rum with her meal and started to tell the pirates stories about her own world. "Where we come from, we have electricity, gas, oil, nuclear energy, solar power, and more to run our world of dishwashers, refrigerators, hairdryers, and so on," she began.

And after Mrs. Morgan told them about skyscrapers, hospitals, schools, libraries, cars, robots, hovercraft, trams, trains, and buses, Master Why told them about rockets, satellites, and space travel. "The Americans put the first man on the moon," he said, "and we have cell phones, computers, and cloud accounts."

The pirates thought Mrs. Morgan and Master Why had fanciful imaginations and were great storytellers, but not for a moment did they believe any of their tales. In turn, they decided to tell Mrs. Morgan and Master Why about killer whales, octopuses big enough to swallow their entire ship, and mean pirates who tortured and killed for information about treasure. Keelhauling, walking the plank, and lashing were just some of the tortures they talked about.

Then one of the pirates said, "Captain Maverick has ordered us to teach you how to tie knots with sailing ropes, repair sails, catch fish, wield a cutlass, and throw a dagger."

"He did, did he," said Mrs. Morgan. "Well, I will *not* accept any order to wield cutlasses and throw daggers. That's dangerous. And anyway, I'm a pacifist."

Master Why blushed and whispered to Mrs. Morgan, "Mom, we're pirates now and must live by their ways. Besides, I'm taller and stronger than my real age."

Mrs. Morgan grumbled, took another swig of rum, and muttered, "I wish I could hand off this decision to your father. He'd know what to do."

Although Mrs. Morgan saw the pirates as an unruly lot, she quickly developed a liking for them, and for their code of ethics and rules. "They don't read books, Saul ... I mean, Master Why," she said in a disapproving voice. "But they do have an admirable code. I'm glad to know that Captain Maverick looks after his injured or sick crew members."

Hawkeye had shown them an impressive scroll:

Pirate Code of the Golden Retriever

1. Every crew member gets an equal share of all treasure. Except Captain Maverick gets three (3) shares. Two (2) shares for himself and one (1) share for injured or sick crew members.

2. Any crew member injured in battle and losing, eye, limb or killed will have access to Captain Maverick's third (3rd) share at the Captain's discretion.

3. No gambling is allowed on board. Punishment is keelhauling.

4. No fighting between crew members allowed. Punishment twenty (20) lashings.

5. No stealing allowed. Punishment—walk the plank.

6. Death to any crew member who runs from a battle or keeps secrets.

7. All weapons must be kept clean & ready for use. Punishment—marooned without food or water.

8. In voting matters every crew member has one (1) equal vote.

9. Captain Maverick has final say on all matters.

"You do not have to sign the pirate code because you are visitors on board and will not get a share of the treasure," Hawkeye had told Mrs. Morgan and Master Why. "But you must honor the pirate code whenever possible," he added.

Mrs. Morgan pondered, "I wonder how the pirate code relates to twenty-first-century life?"

Meanwhile, Master Why thought, "What if mom and dad developed a code for the household chores back home?" This was one thought he would not share with either of his parents. The last thing Master Why wanted was to give them ideas and find himself being keelhauled for not doing the dishes or putting the trash out on time!

The pirates soon learned that while Mrs. Morgan had some strange ways, she meant well and had a good nature. In some ways, it seemed that the pirates and Master Why were more accepting of each other's differences than Mrs. Morgan was. Nevertheless, as time went by, she settled into life on board, and it was hard to see her as a twenty-first-century person anymore. She began to relish her role as a pirate and even drank a little rum from time to time.

Master Why was surprised to learn that after one or two rums Mrs. Morgan was quite an entertaining storyteller. He thought, "The next time I want a story, I must remember to give her some rum. Who knows what secrets she might let slip."

Chapter Four: Scurvy

 Mrs. Morgan changed after Red Beard died. Named for his red beard and bald head, the deck hand had taken ill the day after the feast. Usually a jovial pirate who loved to dance, he could not get out of his hammock. In the daylight, he looked seedy and gray. Peg-legged Cook, who doubled as the ship's doctor because he was good with a knife, told Captain Maverick that Red Beard was dying of scurvy.

The closer Red Beard got to death, the more time Mrs. Morgan spent with him, trying to make him as comfortable as possible. Cook hovered over them like a bad smell, sharpening his knife in case his services were needed.

He really got on Mrs. Morgan's nerves and she told him so: "You're behaving like a bloodthirsty leech, Cook. Get out of here and let me tend to Red Beard."

Cook, not known for taking orders from any woman, left without more than a sigh.

Mrs. Morgan thought, "I wish I was Lisa again, back in the twenty-first century, so I could get Red Beard admitted to a hospital where he could be saved." But she knew she was in a very different world now and needed to follow the pirates' ways.

Master Why continued with his questions. His mind was like a sponge, always soaking up all the information he could get his hands on and wanting answers to as many questions as he could ask. "Why is Cook always called Cook? Doesn't he have a name? How did he get his peg leg? Why doesn't he like women much? And why does he like knives so much?" (Both Popeye and Diego could usually be found near Cook because he often gave them scraps of food. But should they misbehave, Cook was quick to wield his knives. And they knew it!)

He turned to Hawkeye, who patiently answered, "Cook is called Cook because he never knew his real name. When he was a cabin boy, he was shot in his left leg by another pirate. Soon his leg turned a funny color and looked gangrenous. The ship's doctor said it had to be amputated, or he might die of infection. Unfortunately, the doctor had a weakness for rum. Instead of giving Cook the rum as an anesthetic, he drank it himself. The rum confused his brain, and he amputated the wrong leg. Fortunately for Cook, his injured leg healed, or he would be legless today.

Since then, Cook developed a disliking for doctors and surgeons. Oddly enough, he also developed a liking for knives and amputations."

Master Why was surprised by Hawkeye's answers and temporarily ran out of questions. But he made the following mental note: "Remember to smell the breath of any surgeon who comes my way."

When Red Beard finally died, Captain Maverick ordered, "Burial at sea, high noon." The sails were lowered, and the black flag of death was raised for all to see. Master Why badgered Captain Maverick with seemingly endless questions: "Why did Red Beard die? What is scurvy? How did Red Beard catch scurvy? Could I catch scurvy? Why does he have to be buried at sea? Why was he wrapped up in sailcloth? Where is his coffin? Why are the pirates singing a sad song?"

"Master Why! Why, why, why so many questions!" Captain Maverick blurted.

"Because I'm a kid, Captain Maverick, and that's what kids do when they don't understand something," responded Master Why.

Captain Maverick rolled his eyes. But without losing his cool, he patiently answered all of Master Why's questions.

Throughout the burial, Popeye squawked, "Dead

Beard, dead Beard." Afterward the atmosphere on the ship was somber. Some pirates were sad because a friend and crewmate had died, some scared that they could also die the same way. And some pirates were sad and scared at the same time.

Soon enough, life on the *Golden Retriever* returned to normal, with the ship back on course for the Cerebellum Islands. Hawkeye vigilantly scoured the horizon with his telescope, watching for enemy pirate ships, and made sure the pirates regularly practiced their safety procedures and fighting skills. Captain Maverick checked their course and kept the ship's log up to date.

But there was one big difference. The upper deck was now littered with wooden boxes of soil, filled with growing citrus fruit and vegetables. After Red Beard died, Mrs. Morgan had convinced Captain Maverick to sail to the nearest island, where she oversaw the pirates as they built large wooden boxes. Mrs. Morgan knew that citrus fruit and fresh vegetables were needed to stop the rest of the pirates from succumbing to scurvy.

While the boxes were being built, Mrs. Morgan wandered around the island collecting fruit seeds and vegetable roots. She urged Cook to compost the vegetable peelings so they could be added to the soil in the tubs as fertilizer.

Cook was not impressed and said so: "Mrs. Morgan, a fine lady you seem to be. But a meddling lady in my galley I cannot stand to see."

It took Captain Maverick's intervention before a compromise could be found. In the process, Mrs. Morgan convinced the captain to start morning exercise classes on the top deck. "Do you believe it!" exclaimed Master Why. Diego took to watching the exercise routine from the closest lookout and mimicking the pirates' funny movements and grunting sounds. Cook was amused and managed to escape the routine in exchange for finally agreeing with Mrs. Morgan to compost the peelings and leftover vegetables.

Master Why had more questions for Hawkeye. "Why do we have to eat rotten food?"

"Well, Master Why, before leaving port, pirate ships usually stock up with fresh fruit and vegetables, water, salted meat, salted fish, pickled anythings and pickled everthings, chickens for laying eggs, and cows for their milk. As the food loses its freshness—"

"You mean goes rotten," interrupted Master Why.

Hawkeye smiled and continued his explanation. "We also stock up on herbs and spices. These we use to disguise the taste of the food as it loses its freshness. Sometimes we drink a little rum to help wash our food down."

This time, Master Why smiled.

"We do get some fresh food along the way," continued Hawkeye. "When the chickens run out of feed and stop laying eggs, we eat the chickens. And when the cows run out of feed and stop producing milk, we eat the cows. Sometimes we catch turtles and other sea life, which is a pleasant change."

"Back where I come from, we have refrigerators to keep our food fresh," said Master Why.

"What are refrigerators?" asked Hawkeye.

"Kind of like big boxes with cold air inside them," said Master Why.

Hawkeye smiled and thought, "This boy is full of fanciful stories. I wonder where he gets his ideas from."

It was bad enough for Mrs. Morgan seeing her pet chickens eaten after they stopped laying eggs. But she was so relieved that she had not allowed the pirates to take her house cow on the journey because she knew that Bessie would have been eaten as well when she stopped producing milk.

With the *Golden Retriever* one crew member short due to Red Beard's death, Captain Maverick asked Mrs. Morgan and Master Why to help out. Mrs.

Morgan's new job was helping Cook in both the galley and the infirmary. This was to be a challenging arrangement for Cook because he was not used to working with women.

Master Why's new job was sweeping the forequarter of the upper deck, and winding up and storing spare sailing ropes. One day rolled into the next without much variation in the routine of early morning exercises, washing decks, checking rigs, hoisting and lowering sails, repairing sails, tending the dirt boxes, eating, sleeping, and most important, storytelling. Storytelling was one way pirates shared their knowledge, made sense of their lives, and understood the world. However, their next adventure was a story most pirates would not want to experience!

Chapter Five: Whales Ahoy

 "Whales ahoy," shouted Hawk-eye. On the horizon, he had spotted a pod of whales accompanied by a school of dolphins. "Suggest we change course and follow the whales and dolphins, Captain," said Hawkeye, with a glint in his eye. Hawkeye and Captain Maverick shared a love of sea creatures, adventures, and fun, so Captain Maverick was quick to order, "Prepare to come about and give chase to those there whales forward of portside."

Hawkeye's heart and mind raced just like Saul's had when he saw the pirate ship through his kitchen window. Most of the crew shared his excitement.

With her sails fully hoisted and bulging with wind, the Golden Retriever darted through the waves like a lion chasing a gazelle. Unfortunately, mayhem overtook excitement and common sense. In their haste to catch up to the whales and dolphins, the pirates sailed the Golden Retriever smack-dab into the middle of the pod, startling some of the whales.

One of the startled whales responded by ramming the hull of the Golden Retriever.

From the galley where he was preparing dinner, Cook shouted, "Water, water, there is water everywhere." Instinctively, Captain Maverick knew the cause of the water in the galley.

The whale's massive thud had split the wooden hull beneath the waterline, and they were taking on water at an alarmingly fast rate. Popeye squawked, "Sinking ship Maverick, sinking ship Maverick." Captain Maverick barked a series of orders starting with: "Split hull below waterline! Start emergency procedures now!" Like a well-oiled machine, pirates ran about doing all sorts of jobs to save the ship.

Mrs. Morgan and Master Why froze with fear. They had no idea what to do or how to help. And this was no time for Master Why's questions, except for one: "Mom, will we die?"

"I have no idea. Let's watch and see what happens," was her response.

As the Golden Retriever took on water to the sinking point, some of the pirates were repairing the major crack from both inside the ship and over the side under the waterline. Others were frantically trying to bail the water out faster than it was coming in. Survival was looking unlikely, and the Golden Re-

triever seemed destined for the seabed way below.

Neither Captain Maverick nor Hawkeye had time to stop and explain what was going on to Mrs. Morgan and Master Why. The pirates continued caulking the cracks with waxed rope, using special chisels and hammers.

Finally, more water got bailed out than came on board. As dusk settled, Hawkeye reported, "We'll sleep in dry hammocks tonight, Captain." Although close to exhaustion, the crew found the energy to cheer loudly. For two days, the repairs continued until all the water was bailed out and the ship was safe and ready to continue on to the Cerebellum Islands.

Throughout the ordeal, Master Why had watched in awe, as his questions piled up. This was his first near-death experience, and he had a lot on his mind. In significant ways, Master Why's view of what was important and what was not so important in life had changed. He was one of those kids who needed to talk when he had to sort stuff out, so he turned to Mrs. Morgan. "Mom, we could have died at sea. Do you realize that?"

"Yes. But we didn't," replied Mrs. Morgan.

"Mom! I mean, Mrs. Morgan!" said Master Why.

"Yes, Saul," she replied.

"Would it be okay if we just called each other Master Why and Mrs. Morgan? After all, we *are* pirates now."

"Yes, Saul ... I mean, Master Why. That's fine."

"Mrs. Morgan?"

"What is it, Master Why?"

"Well, if we had died, do you think dad would have known that I love him?"

"Yes, Master Why. Your dad knows that you love him," said Mrs. Morgan.

"That's good," replied Master Why. He was silent for a moment, then asked, "Mrs. Morgan, do you think dad knows that I'm sorry for all the fuss I made about chores and keeping my room clean?"

"Yes, Master Why. Dad knows you are sorry and that you were just a kid trying to make sense of your world."

"How do you know, Mrs. Morgan?"

"I just do. Moms and dads know these things. That's why we are called mom and dad."

"Well, Mrs. Morgan, now that I know dad loves me even when I refuse to do the chores or clean my bedroom, I see no reason to do either anymore," said Master Why, with a mischievous look in his eyes.

Mrs. Morgan laughed but, wisely, said nothing.

"If we had died, Mrs. Morgan, what would you have missed the most?"

"I would have missed you, dad, our family, and my friends," said Mrs. Morgan.

"I guess people are more important than possessions," said Master Why.

"Yes, Master Why. A healthy respect for the forces of Mother Nature is also important in the living world," she added.

"I can see why," replied Master Why. "Mrs. Morgan?"

"Yes, Master Why?"

"I think we are still alive because the crew worked like a team."

"Uh-huh," said Mrs. Morgan.

"I watched them, and it reminded me of my basketball team back home. Our coach often told us that ball hogs don't win games. Committed teams win games. I think it was the crew working as a committed team that saved our lives," said Master Why.

"Hmm," said Mrs. Morgan.

"Now I understand why Captain Maverick runs so many rigorous training exercises on board his ship," said Master Why.

"Any more questions, Master Why?" asked Mrs. Morgan.

"That's all for now," answered Master Why.

Sinking ships and dangerous adventures were nothing new to the pirates; much of their life was about survival, adventure, and fun. "Or is it adventure and fun followed by survival?" thought Saul. Having survived the near sinking of the *Golden Retriever*, the pirates were ready to again focus on their journey to the Cerebellum Islands.

En route, Captain Maverick finally gave in to Mrs. Morgan's enthusiasm, charismatic charm, and well-reasoned arguments. "Yes, you have my permission to teach my crew how to read and write," he said. Not surprisingly, Mrs. Morgan was a bit like Master Why when it came to using her infectious enthusiasm to get people on board with her ideas.

On calm days, Mrs. Morgan had the crew on the top deck learning the alphabet and the times tables. Eventually, she had the pirates writing about their adventures and writing letters to their loved ones back home.

Although Mrs. Morgan had to spend a lot of time and energy convincing Captain Maverick to make changes aboard his ship, he quite enjoyed her attention, ideas, and even making some of her chang-es. "It's good to have a woman on board, even though she always wants to change everything," he thought. Some nights he went to sleep wondering, "When I wake up tomorrow morning, what changes will Mrs. Morgan want to make?"

Chapter Six: Are We There Yet?

 Just short of sunrise, Master Why woke up to discover that Mother Nature had changes of her own in mind. Doors banged, shutters rattled, and the wind howled.

Captain Maverick shouted, "We're entering a storm! Batten the hatches, secure the ship's provisions, and stow away anything not secured on the top deck." He knew that the masts were at risk of snapping if he entered the storm with all the sails hoisted, so "Lower all top sails" was the next order he issued. He wanted to limit the *Golden Retriever*'s speed so he could manage it better throughout the storm.

The wind blew furiously, and the waves grew to the size of eighteen-story buildings. The salt spray thrown by the ship's carving through the waves hit Master Why's face so hard that it became red and sore. Even his eyes stung. As the *Golden Retriever* rolled and pitched wildly, Master Why worried that the ship might capsize, leaving them all to drown. Seeing the monstrous waves crash over the bow was a sight he would never forget.

Captain Maverick and Hawkeye were too preoccupied with safely navigating the *Golden Retriever* through the storm to engage with Master Why's usual questions, and he knew it. For once, he was silent.

To make matters worse, it rained and rained. And rained! At times it was hard to tell the difference between the rain and the sea spray. One day, it became so cold that snow landed on the deck. There was no sign of the storm's abating. Rather, it grew wilder and more intense.

For his own safety, Hawkeye confined Master Why to quarters during the worst of the storm, which according to Master Why was most of the time. At least he had Diego and Popeye for entertainment. But as time went by, even the monkey and the parrot offered little distraction from the boredom that set in. For the first time, Master Why became homesick and wished he could be safe in his own bed with his favorite books, music, and toys. "If I were home, I could amuse myself with the Internet and my computer games. Here all I have is a monkey, a parrot, a hammock, four walls, a roof, and a floor. Boring," thought Master Why. Even helping dad out with the household chores or doing homework seemed better options than riding out the storm.

Master Why began to spend more time lying in his hammock, daydreaming. A cheeseburger with lettuce, bacon, no tomato, and a side of fries featured in his first dream. "Oops! I almost forgot the soda," he thought.

During one particularly bad period, when Master Why had been confined to his quarters all day, a memory appeared. He recalled the story:

> I'm lying flat on my back in the emergency room at our local hospital, and dad is in the bed next to me. He had been driving me to school. On the way, he stopped the car at a red light. Unfortunately, the truck behind us didn't brake in time and crashed into the back of our car, pushing us into the middle of the intersection. Luckily, the truck driver was okay, and no one else was hurt. But I remember crying, and my neck was sore. Before I knew it, we were both taken to the hospital with suspected whiplash. When we got there, we were fitted with neck braces and told to lie flat on our backs on the hospital beds until a doctor was available to examine us. In the ER, snakebites, heart attacks, and other serious

stuff get treated before whiplash, so we were stuck with a long wait.

I said to dad, "I'm bored."

"So am I," he agreed.

"What can we do to amuse ourselves?" I asked.

"Let's play I Spy," dad suggested.

"How can we play I Spy when all we can see is the ceiling above us?"

"Use your imagination, Saul" was his answer.

Do you believe it? We played for about fifteen minutes without running out of ideas. It was fun!

The memories helped Master Why imagine another activity. He thought, "How many words can I make out of the alphabet, starting with the letter A and going right through to Z?" And hard as it is to believe, Master Why even daydreamed about going to school! "Only to see my friends," he told himself.

Cook was constantly busy, keeping the crew warm with hot broth and awake with strong coffee. Mrs. Morgan had no time to get bored either, as she found herself hard at work in the infirmary, tending to pirates injured by the storm. She told Master

Why, "I've been treating rope burns, whiplash, cuts, bruises, and a few dislocated shoulders." Manning top deck during a major storm was quite a hazardous occupation.

"And I have been bored stiff," replied Master Why.

When Hawkeye finally allowed Master Why back on the top deck, like a man on a mission he headed straight for Captain Maverick at the helm. "Captain Maverick, could you please hurry up the storm and get us to the Cerebellum Islands faster?"

Before Captain Maverick could start to respond, Master Why suggested, "Maybe we should travel by blink-waves?"

Captain Maverick asked, "What are blink-waves?"

"It's all about mind travel. With mind travel, you imagine where you want to be, blink your eyes, and you'll be there straight after."

Captain Maverick pondered the idea of mind travel for a moment, then smiled. "If you travel by blink-waves, what happens to the journey and all the adventures that take place along the way?"

"I don't know," replied Master Why.

"It's the adventures that create excitement and fun. They build character and teach us about life. If you travel by blink-waves, you will miss out on all of these experiences," explained Captain Maverick.

"Hmm ... maybe you're right," said Master Why. But as he wandered off, Master Why secretly wished they could switch to blink-waves and get to the Cerebellum Islands right away. "Even the first man on the moon would have been there and back several times by now," he thought.

A sudden cry of "Man overboard!" startled Master Why from his thoughts. While he was pondering Captain Maverick's comments, a massive wave had hit the wheelhouse at the helm. The captain was instantly swept overboard. At that same moment, one mast broke, and a pirate was hit in the head by a free-swinging boom. It was just as well Master Why had wandered off, or he would have been swept overboard too.

Hawkeye spotted the captain bobbing up and down in the wild ocean. Besides having the eyes of a hawk, Hawkeye could swim as fast as any Olympic swimmer. Thinking on his feet, he tied a rope around his waist and dived into the ocean after Captain Maverick. He would freely have given his own life if it meant saving the life of his captain.

As Popeye squawked, "Dead Maverick, dead Maverick," Hawkeye swam the fastest race of his life. He needed to reach the captain before the rope ran out. "Without the rope, we will both die," thought Hawkeye.

This was no swimming pool race. It was a race through some of the roughest oceans of the world. Back on board, Cook, who shared Hawkeye's love of Captain Maverick, momentarily considered what life would look like without the captain. His eyes swelled with emotion, and tears clouded his view. Another wave hit the deck and snapped him out of these thoughts. He ran to the helm and took charge of the *Golden Retriever*, steering her toward the captain and Hawkeye.

"Captain," yelled Hawkeye repeatedly when his head cleared the swell of the waves. Captain Maverick did not respond. The more Hawkeye yelled without a reply, the more convinced he was that the captain had drowned. "Popeye was right when he squawked, 'Dead Maverick, dead Maverick'," thought Hawkeye.

Just as the rope was about to run out, Hawkeye found himself on top of the captain. He grabbed hold of him and said, "I'm here, Captain. You'll be safe now," but Captain Maverick did not respond. The rope snapped tight, and Hawkeye realized that his beloved captain's body was limp. The thought of Captain Maverick's being dead was too much for Hawkeye to consider. Instead, he yelled in his loudest of loud voices to the crew of the *Golden Retriever*, "Haul us in and fast!"

In response, the crew heaved and tugged at the rope with all their strength and speed until they had the captain and Hawkeye safely back on board.

The rumor swiftly circulated around the crew: "Captain Maverick is dead." Just then, Mrs. Morgan appeared. She checked the captain's vitals and said, "He's got a pulse, his heart is pumping, he's unconscious, and he's got a belly full of seawater." She applied CPR. Soon the captain regained consciousness and vomited up the seawater. A huge sigh of relief moved through the crew and culminated in cheers of joy. A new rumor was swift to circulate: "Captain Maverick is alive! Mrs. Morgan saved him!"

During the storm, most of the provisions on the upper deck had been swept overboard, including Mrs. Morgan's fruit and vegetable boxes. Still, it was more important to save the captain than Mrs. Morgan's vegetable boxes! Well, Mrs. Morgan was not quite sure at the time ... but that's another story.

Master Why thought the accident with the whale was bad enough, but being stuck in this horrendous storm and almost losing Captain Maverick took the cake, in his opinion. The storm continued for several more days. The crew became dog-tired and low in spirits. Eventually fatigue took over and all fell asleep, except for Captain Maverick and Cook. The captain remained alert at the helm and focused on steering the ship through the storm and on to the Cerebellum Islands.

Captain Maverick was the sort of captain who believed it his duty to look after his crew, navigate his ship safely, and, should his ship break up and sink, go down with it. Although a great adventurer and a lover of fun, he was a responsible man with a solid set of ethics. Even so, he fought feelings of tiredness. He was not going to let sleep deprivation take control of his body. It was Cook who helped keep the captain awake with hot coffee and dry bread. It was at times like these that the captain and Cook reaffirmed their special bond. Cook liked caring for the captain, and the captain liked being cared for by Cook.

Exhaustion finally set in, and Captain Maverick's brain started to play games with his thoughts. In his fatigued state, he felt a false sense of power, and his decision-making abilities were clouded by feelings of euphoria and numbness.

When Cook screeched, "Captain, Captain, it's stopped raining," his loud voice shocked Captain Maverick's brain back into rational thinking, and the captain noticed that the wind had lessened. He gave Cook a gigantic smile and said, "She's all yours."

With that instruction, he collapsed to the deck and fell fast asleep. Cook quickly made the captain comfortable and then took control of the helm.

When the captain, the crew, Master Why, and Mrs. Morgan woke up, they saw Cook fast asleep bent over the helm. The seas were calm, the sun shone brightly, and there were birds in the sky, suggesting they might be close to land. As it turned out, Captain Maverick and Cook had brilliantly navigated the *Golden Retriever* safely (though some would argue dangerously) to their destination, the Cerebellum Islands.

Captain Maverick declared, "Breakfast—a feast and celebration!"

Cook liked the idea of the celebration. "But what will we do for food, Captain?" he asked. "There is not much left to eat on board."

With a mischievous glint in his eyes, the captain replied, "Yes there is. Ask for a volunteer." Cook looked horrified and then laughed. Knowing they were close to land, Captain Maverick dispatched a team of pirates to row ashore and return with a wild pig. To the cooked wild pig, they added what was left of their food, rotten and all. They even found some rum in the captain's private stash.

Popeye squawked, "Pig Maverick, pig Maverick,"

and the crew sang, "We made it, we made it, we made it to the Cerebellum Islands!" Not one crew member was missing as a consequence of the storm, but there were quite a few injuries that Mrs. Morgan had been dealing with. She did manage to keep Cook and his sharp knife out of the infirmary with this promise: "I give you my solemn word that I will let you know if any of the injured pirates need an amputation or any knife work of any kind."

With a beaming smile, Captain Maverick held a mug of rum in one hand and a succulent piece of roast pig in the other. He turned to Master Why and asked, "Is the destination worth the adventure?"

Master Why returned the captain's smile and said, "*Yes!*"

"Tomorrow the search for the cave begins," said the captain.

Chapter Seven: The Black Dragon

"Could that be a ship on the horizon?" thought Hawkeye. While the celebrations were in full swing, Hawkeye had become aware of a large moving object far on the horizon. He grabbed his telescope and carefully studied it. "No doubting it. It's the *Black Dragon*," Hawkeye muttered to himself.

The *Black Dragon* could be likened to anyone's worst nightmare and its captain, Captain Hammerhead, held the dubious honor of having sunk the most ships of any captain in the history of piracy.

Throughout the long journey, Hawkeye had kept a close watch out for any other pirate ships that might be following them, yet he had seen nothing until this morning. Hawkeye was aware that Captain Hammerhead knew about the secret legend and would do anything to get hold of the map and the key. He would even sink the *Golden Retriever* with its entire crew, if it meant getting the map and key. Quickly, Hawkeye drew Captain Maverick's attention, and they both went below deck.

"Are you sure it's the *Black Dragon*?" asked Captain Maverick.

"As sure as my mother's name is Agnes," responded Hawkeye.

"Hmm …" said the captain.

"What are our options, Captain?"

"Rather limited."

"Maybe it's time to skip to the next chapter," suggested Hawkeye with a wry smile.

The captain laughed and said, "Master Why had a similar idea during the storm. He wanted to travel by blink-waves. I told him he'd miss all the adventure and fun."

"I guess so," said Hawkeye.

"Let's focus on the job ahead. I think the *Black Dragon* has been stalking us since well before we entered the storm. That makes me think Captain Hammerhead knew about our plans well in advance."

"I guess so, Captain. With its seventy-two cannons to our thirty-six, the *Black Dragon* has a superior fighting power. And its crew will show no mercy in battle. We are in serious trouble," said Hawkeye.

"I know," said Captain Maverick, "but I have a plan.

When forced to fight a shark, one must become a fiercer shark or die."

"I agree," said Hawkeye.

"Surrendering to torture and sure death thereafter is not an option. I will become a white pointer shark and outsmart the hammerhead shark."

Hawkeye smiled and looked at the captain. "I knew you would think of something." They both knew that if the secret map got into Captain Hammerhead's hands, he would end up with the Power of the Cranium and probably reek havoc on the world.

When Master Why heard the news, he asked Hawkeye, "How did Captain Hammerhead get his name?"

Hawkeye said, "The story goes like this: While the crew of the *Black Dragon* was robbing a merchant vessel in shark-infested waters, Captain Hammerhead was hit by gunfire and fell overboard. He was attacked by three hammerhead sharks simultaneously, and he fought them all off single-handedly."

"Really?" said Master Why.

"Yes, really. He killed all three sharks," said Hawkeye.

"I've heard of one man fighting off a single shark, but never one man fighting off three sharks at the same time," said Master Why.

"Now you know where Captain Hammerhead got his name—and why he is the most feared pirate of all time," said Hawkeye.

Outsmarting and outmaneuvering Captain Hammerhead was to be the challenge of a lifetime for Captain Maverick. "I have a fallback plan," he thought. "I can be the fastest gazelle and outrun the lion. She has twice as many cannons as we do, which makes her heavier and slower."

Confident of the *Golden Retriever*'s speed, and known to be an excellent tactician, Captain Maverick devised a highly risky plan. The orders began. "Load all the cannons and pistols ready for use, and place spare ammunition in piles next to each cannon. Cook, hand out cutlasses and daggers to every crew member, including Mrs. Morgan and Master Why. Set the upper deck to look like a disaster zone"—an easy task after the storm they had just survived—"rip a few sails, and scatter them so some hang over the side of the ship. Open every third and seventh cannon door, and leave the rest closed. Upon my order to attack, open the rest, roll out all the cannons, and fire them repeatedly."

The crew got to work following Captain Maverick's orders. To the debris left from the storm, they added miscellaneous items, clothing, and stores strewn everywhere on the upper deck. They had to work fast and out of sight of the *Black Dragon*'s crew, who they knew would be watching them closely, so they crept around the upper deck on all fours.

Without making himself visible to the *Black Dragon*, Captain Maverick toured the upper deck. He satisfied himself that his ship did in fact look like a total disaster zone. He was pleased that his orders had been completed before the crew of the *Black Dragon* would notice the changes.

"Raise the anchor. Then all hands below deck," was Captain Maverick's next order. He wanted his ship to drift aimlessly and look lifeless. Below deck, he briefed his crew about the battle plans. Popeye squawked, "War Maverick, war Maverick." The last thing Captain Maverick wanted was for Popeye to squawk as the *Black Dragon* drew alongside, so he quickly muzzled the parrot. Surprisingly, it would be Diego, not Popeye, who put the whole plan at risk.

As the *Black Dragon* came within clear visual range, it looked huge and mean. And well, it *was* huge and mean. All black and ominous in appearance, it bore a hammerhead shark's head on its bow. Even its sails were black and threatening. Through his telescope, Hawkeye could see Captain Hammerhead at the helm. One hand clasped a walking stick (the result of a shark fight) and the other a telescope. He was not as tall as Captain Maverick, or even Hawkeye, but he was solid. He wore a smart black-braided captain's uniform and a black pirate hat adorned with fancy feathers and jewels, and had a long, graying beard.

Captain Maverick ordered, "Remain silent but ready to attack." His crew were both excited and anxious. Their adrenalin was pumping. The captain whispered, "Do not move or make a sound until I give the order." The smell of nervous perspiration permeated the gunnery. "Timing and surprise are the essence of my plan." But the question bothering the captain was this: What would he do with Diego?

In a quiet whisper, Master Why asked Captain Maverick, "Why is the *Black Dragon* named the *Black Dragon* when it has a hammerhead shark on its bow? Shouldn't it be named the *Black Hammerhead* or something like that?"

"Master Why, that's a good question. After the battle, I'll give you the answer. Now silence and no more questions," said Captain Maverick.

Soon the *Black Dragon* was within firing range; it was a frightening sight. Captain Hammerhead ordered, "Prepare to fire!" and all its cannon doors swung open. As the cannons rolled forward, Captain Hammerhead became spooked by his own questions: Why was the *Golden Retriever* drifting aimlessly? Where were the captain and crew? And why were ripped sails hanging over the side?

He did not see any adventure or excitement in firing on a lifeless ship. The *Golden Retriever* certainly looked like a disaster zone. "It is most unusual to see a pirate ship drifting idly in the middle of nowhere," he thought. "Could it be jinxed? Could it be inhabited by ghosts?" If Captain Hammerhead had one weakness, it was his fear of ghosts. Would you believe it, a grown man who could single-handedly wrestle and kill three sharks scared of ghosts? Well, he was. His doubt grew, and his judgment suffered. "Maybe I should give the *Golden Retriever* a wide berth and head for the island beyond."

Ultimately, his curiosity and his compulsive desire for the secret map overtook his fear of ghosts. "Prepare to throw the grappling hooks and board the *Golden Retriever*," ordered Captain Hammerhead. In heading to the upper deck to follow his orders, his crew left the cannons below deck unattended.

Meanwhile, back on board the *Golden Retriever*, all was deathly quiet. Captain Maverick and his crew remained silent and ready for battle. All except for that naughty monkey Diego who, ignoring Captain Maverick's orders, continued to play hide-and-seek.

As the *Black Dragon* drew closer, Captain Hammerhead and his crew were struck by the eeriness of the situation, as if they expected ghosts to appear on the deck of the *Golden Retriever*.

Captain Maverick's crew remained silent and still, but battle ready. Suddenly, Diego popped out with a "Boo!" which the crew almost misinterpreted as their captain's order to fire. Diego's "Boo" gave Captain Maverick the fright of his life. He thought, "That monkey is going to be the death of all of us." Urgently, he whispered, "Catch and silence Diego!"

In response, Cook appeared with one of his sharp knives. Diego knew that Cook would not hesitate to use his knife if Captain Maverick gave the order. Cook whispered, "Diego, come here or eat my knife." A fearful expression gripped the monkey's face, and without hesitation he followed Cook's instructions. Cook quickly muzzled Diego and put him in his cage. "Phew, that was close," said Captain Maverick.

As the *Black Dragon* entered the point of no return, Hawkeye pestered Captain Maverick: "Give the order to fire."

"No," said Captain Maverick. "Surprise is our greatest weapon. We must wait until the last possible moment."

Next Captain Hammerhead ordered the grappling hooks thrown over the *Golden Retriever*'s deck. That was the signal Captain Maverick had been waiting for. He ordered, "Fire all starboard cannons in rapid succession—now! Open the rest of the cannon doors, roll out the cannons, and fire them in rapid succession as well!"

Captain Maverick's crew sprang into action and followed his orders in every detail. The noise was deafening, and the air smelled of gunpowder as the cannons fired repeatedly.

Captain Hammerhead and his crew were completely taken by surprise. The *Black Dragon* was badly damaged and began taking on water. The battleground was covered in thick dense smoke and fire. Utter confusion reigned on board the *Black Dragon* as its crew tried to figure out what was going on and what to do next.

Captain Maverick continued his relentless attack with all the ferocity he could muster. As half his men boarded the *Black Dragon* and obliterated her crew, the proud captain thought, "Today I am a white pointer who is taking out a hammerhead."

Captain Hammerhead's face turned red and puffy with fury. "I've been outmaneuvered by Captain Maverick. My ship is sinking, and we lost the battle without firing even one cannon," he grumbled. Soon, a loud hissing sound could be heard as the water rose and the *Black Dragon* disappeared into the dark depths of the sea, never to be seen again.

Although Captain Maverick's tactics were brilliant, they were highly risky. That they worked made it possible for this story to be told.

Master Why and Mrs. Morgan watched the battle from the lower deck, where they had been helping the crew reload the cannons and pistols.

"Thank goodness that terrible noise has stopped," said Mrs. Morgan.

"What a shame we didn't get to use our cutlasses and daggers," said Master Why.

"Hmm," said Mrs. Morgan and then she returned to the infirmary to check on the crew members who had been wounded aboard the *Black Dragon*. True to her word, she called to Cook, "Come here and bring your knives." Good for Cook! But not so good for the crew members, who needed a few limbs here and there amputated and a few eye patches fitted.

Hawkeye congratulated Captain Maverick on his wonderful victory and began to count the wounded. The captain was secretly pleased that Mrs. Morgan had convinced him to agree to the morning exercise program and to improving the crew's diet, and he was glad that his crew had slept through the worst of the storm. The combination of these factors pre-pared them very well for the battle they had just won.

"Dead pirates Maverick, dead pirates Maverick"

could be heard as Popeye had his muzzle removed. For Diego's part, he had no idea how close he had come to ruining Captain Maverick's war plan and to eating Cook's knife. After all, he was a monkey and knew nothing of such matters.

Master Why followed Captain Maverick on his rounds as he personally checked the wounded, counted the dead, and looked for any visible damage to the *Golden Retriever*. Naturally, Master Why had a long list of questions, which began with: "Captain Maverick, you promised to tell me why the *Black Dragon* was named the *Black Dragon*?"

"Yes I did, Master Why," said Captain Maverick. "Long before Captain Hammerhead killed those three hammerhead sharks, he named his ship the *Black Dragon* because he believed that ghosts were scared of dragons. He even adorned the bow of his ship with a dragon's head. After killing those sharks, he realized that his ability to kill sharks single-handedly was more fearsome than even dragons. So he changed his name to Captain Hammerhead. He also changed the dragon's head on the bow to the head of a hammerhead shark. It was a good move. Just the sight of that hammerhead was enough to make any ship surrender."

"But why not change the name of his ship to the *Hammerhead*?" asked Master Why.

"Superstition, Master Why. It is considered bad luck to change the name of any pirate ship," said Captain Maverick.

As Master Why pondered this explanation, Captain Maverick got a temporary reprieve from his questions. After a bit, Master Why exclaimed, "So he really traded on fear when he changed his name to Captain Hammerhead!"

"Yes," replied Captain Maverick.

"When will we go ashore and find the Power of the Cranium?" was Master Why's next question.

"Tomorrow. After we have buried the dead at sea and tended to the wounded," answered Captain Maverick.

Chapter Eight: The Cerebellum Island

After a somber burial at sea, the entire crew rowed ashore, except for Diego, Popeye and those injured in the battle. They stayed on board to look after the ship and alert Captain Maverick should anything or anyone unwanted appear on the horizon.

The instructions on Captain Maverick's brown leather map first took the crew high into the mountains, where the air was thin and the vegetation scant. Then they descended into a deep gully, where the air was thick and humid and the vegetation dense. With sweat dripping from his forehead, Captain Maverick ordered rest and water for all.

While they rested, Hawkeye and the captain studied the map carefully, with Master Why peering over their shoulders. The map was very old, and much of the leather was cracked. In places it was hard to understand. Hawkeye said, "According to the map, there should be a cave covered in vines in this gully."

"How do we find it?" asked Master Why.

"To start, we will all spread out and look for vines," said the captain, and then he gave the order. You'd think finding vines in a gully would be easy, but it was a real challenge because this gully was more like a tropical forest than a gully.

When Cook shouted, "Vines over here!" everyone followed his voice, and soon they all stood in front of a massive green wall of vines. The atmosphere was electric.

Master Why turned to Mrs. Morgan. "Do you realize that somewhere behind these vines is a cave, and inside the cave is the greatest treasure of all time?"

"Yes. I'm excited as well," said Mrs. Morgan.

"How do we find the cave behind such a thick and high wall of vines?" asked Master Why. The captain had been pondering the same question.

"That's easy," said Mrs. Morgan. "Pass me a machete, and I'll show you." Hawkeye handed her a machete. She followed the vines to their main roots in the soil and began to cut them free.

"Spread out and do the same as Mrs. Morgan," ordered Captain Maverick.

Back on board the *Golden Retriever* all seemed quiet, and there was no sign of unwanted visitors on the horizon. Popeye and Diego amused themselves annoying the wounded, who were trying to rest and recover.

Soon a shout came from Hawkeye. "Cave door! I've found the cave door!" Within moments, the whole crew was pushing each other aside in their rush to see the door.

"Have you all forgotten your manners?" shouted Captain Maverick. "Clear the way!" Both the captain and Hawkeye walked between the two lines of crew toward the cave door. Naturally, Master Why snuck in behind them.

The cave door was impressive. It stood close to twelve feet high and seven feet wide and was arched at the top. Made of thick wooden beams, it was held together with a steel frame and large steel bolts. "It has certainly been built to last," thought Master Why. It even had a steel combination lock, which was rare in those days.

With great enthusiasm, Captain Maverick removed the key from around his neck. Ceremoniously, he turned to face his crew and announced, "With this key, I hereby open the door to the greatest treasure of all time: the Power of the Cranium." Swiftly, he inserted the key and began to turn it right, then left, then right again and left again. But nothing happened. In the excitement, Captain Maverick had momentarily overlooked the steel combination lock.

As Cook pointed tactfully toward the steel lock, he said, "Let's ram it. No. Let's shoot the locks. No, better still, let's blow it up!"

Captain Maverick smiled, then said, "No."

The entire crew sighed as one, and their excitement seemed crushed by disappointment. Captain Maverick sat down on the ground in front of the cave door and thought. Hawkeye and Master Why did the same.

"Could the answer be on the map?" asked Master Why.

"Good thinking, Master Why," said the captain. Again he unfolded the map, and the three of them studied it in great detail. But still no inspiration appeared. What would Popeye have squawked if he were there? No doubt nothing helpful, so maybe it was just as well he was back on board the *Golden Retriever*.

With despair in his voice, Captain Maverick said to the crew, "Our voyage is in vain if we can't get inside the cave. Any suggestions other than blowing it up?"

"We just need four numbers in the right sequence to open the combination lock. What could they be?"

said Hawkeye.

Suddenly Captain Maverick shouted, "I've got it. It's the longitude and the latitude of the Cerebellum Islands." Master Why had been right. The answer *was* on the leather map. The captain was quick to dial these numbers into the steel combination lock. With a great sigh of relief and much excitement in his voice, Captain Maverick announced, "I have opened the combination lock." His crew cheered loudly.

Again Captain Maverick removed the key from the chain he wore around his neck, this time without any ceremony. He inserted the key and instinctively turned it to the left. "Yes, it works!" he exclaimed.

Next the door opened itself, revealing what can best be described as a most surreal environment. The pirates would not be wrong if they compared it to Mrs. Morgan's and Master Why's fanciful stories, yet it appeared to be as real as the sun rising on a new day.

Captain Maverick ordered, "Hawkeye, on my right; Cook, on my left; Mrs. Morgan and Master Why, behind us. Crew, follow behind."

Entering the cave was overwhelming, an experience unlike any they had ever had. It was scary, because no one knew what dangers lurked inside the cave, and it was exciting, because this was an adventure of a lifetime. There was no human life to be seen, and no animals for that matter. The place was spotlessly clean and well lit.

As Master Why steered Captain Maverick to the left of the entrance, he said in a very excited voice, "Look, Captain! It's a library … and it's filled with books and music. Artwork, too!" His excitement drove his voice higher. "And even games and electronic devices!"

Captain Maverick's eyes were those of a child about to open a big birthday present. "This place is like nothing I have ever seen before. And it smells funny," he said.

"I think it's the cafeteria food you smell," said Master Why, who was quite familiar with the smells of his school cafeteria.

"What's a cafeteria?" asked Captain Maverick.

"One of those over there. Go check it out. It won't hurt you or anything," replied Master Why. When Captain Maverick, Hawkeye, Cook and the crew entered the cafeteria, they found it stocked with healthy food and beverages. Not that they knew what healthy food and beverages were … but that's yet another story.

While the pirates gorged themselves, Master Why and Mrs. Morgan investigated the e-book library.

"Look, Mrs. Morgan. It's just like a regular library bookshelf, except the books are illuminated on a touch screen," said Master Why.

"How does it work?" asked Mrs. Morgan.

"Like this. Touch the book that interests you. Then read the menu that pops up. The menu lets you do almost anything. If you like the book, you can follow the prompts and send it to your cloud account on loan, or you can buy it and have it saved on your cloud account," explained Master Why.

"Wow!" said an awestruck Mrs. Morgan. "A virtual library next to a conventional library. A little music and I'll be in seventh heaven!"

"That's easily fixed. Press the music button on the e-book menu, choose your music, and you'll be totally surrounded by it within a three-foot radius. Nobody outside that radius will be able to hear it," said Master Why, who detested Mrs. Morgan's taste in music.

Mrs. Morgan discovered that the music followed her as she browsed the bookshelves. "This is too much," she thought. "Now I know what seventh heaven feels like."

When Master Why joined the captain and crew in the cafeteria, they looked happy— and they were quite full, even though they had never eaten or drunk food and beverages like these in the past. "Thank goodness milk shakes and muffins are considered healthy food," thought Master Why as he helped himself.

"Master Why, where is the rum kept?" asked Captain Maverick. Popeye certainly would have known what to say, but he was back on board the *Golden Retriever*.

"Libraries don't have rum, Captain Maverick," said Master Why.

"Then I don't like libraries, Master Why," said Captain Maverick. "Anyway, what *are* libraries?" he asked in a loud, belligerent voice.

From outside the cafeteria entrance, Mrs Morgan chimed in, "Libraries are places of adventure, fun, and learning."

Although he actually agreed, Master Why rolled his eyes and thought, "Who is the captain asking, you or me?"

"Hmm," said the captain. "My crew came all this way for the loot. You know, jewels, gold, coins, and trinkets. Not to mention the Power of the Cranium." Then he thought, "Why am I disappointed? What sort of adventure has Atlanticus really sent me on?" Captain Maverick had the greatest respect for the old prophet. And based on that respect, he decided to keep an open mind and continue exploring. Realizing that their whereabouts were more like Master Why's world than his own, he ordered, "Master Why, lead the way."

Master Why's chest almost burst with pride. "I am now a pirate *and* a tour guide," he thought enthusiastically.

Although Master Why shared some of the captain's disappointment, the excitement of the library seemed more interesting. Likewise, Mrs. Morgan was too lost in the excitement of digital books and virtual music to think about loot. And if you think virtual surround music is cool, what about WiFi electricity? Yes, the library had tablet readers that could be recharged with electricity anywhere within the library via WiFi. No more messy leads and portable chargers. "Wow. This place is something else. Virtual music. Virtual electricity. What next," thought Master Why.

The whole cave turned out to be one gigantic bubble surrounded by many smaller connected bubbles, as Master Why and his entourage soon realized. Next they found themselves in the huge main hall, which was made of touch-sensitive glass. Do you believe it? Even the roof and floor were made the same way. Master Why chose to screen *The Battle of Port Royal* in the hope that the captain and his crew would feel more at home with it than with a film foreign to their world. He told them to put on the 3D glasses he had given them, then started the screening. As he did, Master Why worried that the pirates might be freaked out.

Master Why was right. The pirates were freaked out; the notion of moving digital imagery was totally unknown to them. At first they froze and watched in awe. Then they drew their arms, ready for battle. Master Why reassured them, "They're not ghosts, and they won't hurt you. Just watch and enjoy." Interestingly, the pirates trusted Master Why and followed his instructions. Soon they were mesmerized by the action on the screens and even tried to join in.

Now that the pirates had lost their fear of the virtual battle of Port Royal, Master Why took them to explore the smaller bubbles. As they entered the first one, Captain Maverick asked, "What goes on in these bubbles? And why so many?"

"Why so many questions, Captain Maverick?" said Master Why, with a glint of mischief in his eyes.

Captain Maverick smiled and said, "That's what adults do when they don't understand stuff."

They both laughed and then Master Why explained, "This one is a digital bubble for watching movies and documentaries; over there is a reading bubble for quiet reading. There's also a discussion bubble where people can debate their ideas, a private study bubble, a group study bubble, a meditation bubble—"

"A what?" interrupted Captain Maverick.

"Later, Captain Maverick. I'll answer later," replied Master Why. "And there's a storytelling bubble and a gym—"

"A what?" Captain Maverick repeated.

Again Master Why said, "Later, Captain Maverick. I'll answer later." But he never did!

After showing the pirates the indoor swimming pool, hot tubs, ceramics bubble, woodworking bubble, drawing bubble, radio station, recording studio, and much more, Master Why realized that this library had something for almost everyone. The pirates stopped thinking about the loot and began to experience all the cave-library had to offer.

A big feature of the library was its focus on gameplay and experiential learning. It was a place where the past, present, and future could be pondered and understood in relation to each other to some degree. Next they entered a technology bubble. Operated by touch and eye contact, the center could be used for accessing information, making financial transactions, and the like. It was next to the business bubble, which had boring business stuff. Naturally there was a kids' area on the other side of the technology bubble, but nobody in this group seemed interested in kid stuff.

Inside the technology bubble they found an energy center housing many torches. They looked like Olympic torches, except they were made of glass and topped with skulls. Selecting a torch and looking into the skull's eye sockets made a virtual world appear in front of one's eyes. It was awesome. There were time-travel torches, creative-thinking torches, problem-solving torches, brainteaser activity torches, and imagination torches. Yes, besides the cafeteria, the technology bubble was the big draw card. When word spread about the interactive technology torches, all the pirates converged in this bubble.

Although the pirates hadn't entirely forgotten about jewels, gold, and trinkets, they were distracted by the unfamiliar torches. Hawkeye said to Mrs. Morgan, "There must be more."

"I don't know. But I can tell you that jewels, gold, and trinkets are only temporary possessions. They can be taken away from you. But knowledge gained from learning and understanding becomes yours for life and nobody can take that away from you," said Mrs. Morgan.

And as she spoke those words, Mrs. Morgan was struck by a sudden realization: "Now I know how the fable of the gazelle and the lion relates to modern life. It's about knowledge and how to use its power and competitive edge. The people who use their brains in creative and flexible ways are likely to survive and prosper."

Eventually, curiosity overtook awe and caution, and the pirates engaged themselves with everything the technology bubble had to offer. They become totally captivated. Nothing else seemed to exist except adventure, fun, and learning. And the pirates certainly understood the first two.

Chapter Nine: The Secret Scroll

 While his crew was absorbed in the technology bubble, Captain Maverick reflected on what he had seen and experienced since entering the cave. Instinctively, he believed there was something more to discover, so he decided to do a little exploration of his own. "I'm right," he thought, as he came across a silver cylinder mounted horizontally above the entrance to the technology bubble. "Hmm, I wonder what's in that cylinder?"

The captain's heart pounded as he anticipated its contents. Upon removing the cylinder from its resting place, he discovered the words "The Power of the Cranium" etched in black along its underside. "I've found it!" he thought. "Yes, I have the Power of the Cranium right in my hands. Atlanticus will be so pleased with me."

Without delay, he unscrewed the cap and to his excitement found a tightly rolled scroll. Three questions raced through his mind: "I wonder what's on it? I wonder what it says? And is it a treasure map?" The scroll looked, felt, and smelled like cured pig-skin. Rapid-fire thoughts popped into the captain's head: "It must be a map. Should I open it? What did Atlanticus really mean when he asked me to acquire the source of the Power of the Cranium? Okay, I will seal it back in its cylinder and hand it to Atlanticus. No, I won't." And with those words, the captain proceeded to unroll the scroll.

His heart was racing like a gazelle, and perspiration began to drip onto the scroll. To his total surprise, Captain Maverick discovered that written into the scroll was the information to help brains grow and develop their competitive edges. He stood still like a stunned mullet as he read:

The Power of the Cranium

1. The brain is an organ born to learn, manage the body, adapt to change, and fight for the eternal survival of the human species.

2. The brain is an expert problem-solver, and the source of imagination, ideas, innovativeness, creative thinking, and emotion.

3. The brain is a source of much fun, excitement, and pleasure.

4. The brain controls everything you say, do, hear, feel, smell, see, and taste.

5. The brain is competitive in nature and constantly changing.

6. Healthy brains require adequate sleep, nutritious food, exercise, and a fit body.

7. Human brains learn in many ways that include the active engagement in game-play, storytelling, listening, reading, writing, comparing, contrasting, thinking, repetition, mistakes, exploration, reflection, and much more.

8. You can influence how your brain changes and what it learns.

9. Always protect your brain when playing sports.

10. Using your brain effectively is your competitive edge.

The captain quickly assembled his crew and read the scroll aloud. Master Why was not surprised to learn that the brain was the greatest treasure of all time. But he was surprised and excited to learn that brainpower was just as important as physical strength, if not more so. Of course, strong muscles were important. Yet, the real power and competitive edge came from the brain and knowing how to use it. After all, Captain Maverick had used his brainpower to outwit Captain Hammerhead. Now Master Why was becoming aware that learning was so much more than he ever realized.

As for the captain and rest of the crew, they felt like fish out of water. They had not seen nor heard anything like this before, and their imaginations did not seem capable of comprehending or envisioning such a world. Again, Captain Maverick was like a kid needing to ask lots of questions about things he did not understand. Master Why gladly obliged and had enormous pleasure answering the captain's many questions. Captain Maverick now realized that the scroll was the treasure he must take to Atlanticus.

Chapter Ten: Mom's Practical Side

 It had been a long journey and —as you probably expected— Mrs. Morgan's practical side finally kicked back in. She became more like Saul's mom. "Saul, it's time to go home," she said.

"I'm not Saul. I'm Master Why, pirate and crew member of the *Golden Retriever*," responded Master Why.

"Okay, okay. You are Master Why. But Master Why, it's time for the two of us to return to twenty-first-century life, to my husband, your dad," said Mrs. Morgan.

"No. Not now. I'm having too much fun," said Master Why.

Now the tables had turned. Mrs. Morgan wanted to go home, and Master Why wanted to stay. What could Mrs. Morgan say or do to convince Master Why it was time to leave? She thought hard and then, in despair, she played the love-guilt card. "Master

Why, your dad loves you. He's lonely, and he misses you terribly. You must go home and see him," said Mrs. Morgan, feeling guilty even as she spoke.

"No, he doesn't. He's fast asleep and thinks this is all a dream," responded Master Why.

Mrs. Morgan was temporarily lost for words, but she was secretly pleased that her guilt trip had not worked because she did not like that sort of thing. Next she turned to face her son so that their eyes locked, and in her most charming of charming voices said, "Master Why, I love you. You are the best. Will you please come home with me?"

And it was those words that did the trick. Master Why responded in a most caring and loving way and said, "You're right, Mrs. Morgan. It's time to go home."

Mrs. Morgan and Master Why had the choice of sailing home with the pirates or taking the time-travel torch, which Master Why nicknamed Blink-waves. Mrs. Morgan turned to Captain Maverick and asked, "What will you do if Master Why and I take the time-travel torch?"

"I think we will stay here awhile and grasp the power of the cave, give the other torches a whirl, and then take the scroll to Atlanticus in Mosquito Bay," answered Captain Maverick.

With this matter resolved, Master Why and Mrs. Morgan said their good-byes, and then Master Why went over to collect the time-travel torch. As he did so, all hell broke loose. The sound of gunfire echoed throughout the technology bubble, followed by the smell of gunpowder and smoke.

You guessed it! Captain Hammerhead and six of his crew had survived the sea battle by jumping overboard and swimming ashore. From a discreet distance, they had followed Captain Maverick and his crew to the cave. And when Captain Maverick and his crew were fully absorbed with the activities in the technology bubble, they attacked.

This time, Captain Maverick and his crew had been caught unprepared, and now Captain Hammerhead had the upper hand—but not for long, thanks to some stunning work by Cook, who never left the galley without a knife, or several knives for that matter, and was always looking for an opportunity to use them.

In a flash, Cook spun around to face Captain Hammerhead and in the same motion threw a knife. It whistled through the air and landed in Captain Hammerhead's heart. As Captain Hammerhead fell to the ground, Captain Maverick's crew overpowered the remaining pirates.

During the fast and furious battle, the time-travel

torch was hit by gunfire. "Oh dear," sighed a forlorn Mrs. Morgan. "I want to go home to dad, and now it will take almost a year by sea."

Although Master Why had been having the time of his life, at another level he was also missing his dad, his home, and his friends. In a positive and cheery voice, he said, "It's okay, Mrs. Morgan. I'll find a way of getting Blink-waves to work." And with those words he began tinkering with the skull that topped the torch.

Soon enough, he shouted, "Quick, Mrs. Morgan, quick! Blink-waves is working, and it's time to go. Wrap your arms around my waist."

Mrs. Morgan quickly did what she was told. As Master Why locked his eyes with the eye sockets of the skull and thought of their destination, Captain Maverick and his entire crew cheered and waved goodbye.

"Yikes" was the first word Mrs. Morgan spoke as she realized Blink-waves had taken them into the middle of a battlefield in the Second World War.

"Duck for cover!" were Master Why's first words.

"Master Why, you must have thought of the wrong location back in the technology center. How are we going to get out of here alive?" asked Mrs. Morgan.

"I have no idea. Stay close to me, and my creative

thinking will come up with something," responded Master Why. True to his word, Master Why did come up with something—and not a moment too soon, as three mean-looking tanks were headed their way. In a flash, Blink-waves did its thing and took them out of harm's way. But for how long was the question?

Knowing that Blink-waves had been damaged, Mrs. Morgan was worried about where it would take them next. "Will we end up in a country populated by cannibals? On a space ship heading toward Mars? Or maybe back in the Wild West?" were the questions going through Mrs. Morgan's mind.

Master Why's mind was more focused on adventure, and he did not share Mrs. Morgan's fears. Nonetheless, he was hoping it would be to see his dad.

Chapter Eleven: The Kitchen Table

"You really are the best, Saul," were his mom's first words to Saul as, to their pleasant surprise, they found themselves back in their house, sitting at their kitchen table.

As she contentedly sipped her coffee, Saul gazed at the torch. His mind was miles away and focused on more journeys. But this time, they had to include his dad. "I can't wait to tell my friends at school about my adventure," he thought. Suddenly the time-travel torch started to vibrate on the table. Before his astounded eyes, the torch shattered like a broken windshield. All that remained was a pile of sand. Saul and his mom gazed at it sadly.

Just then, dad woke up. Looking unshaven, sleepy, and disheveled in wrinkled PJs, he made his way to the kitchen via the bathroom for a cup of coffee. As on many other mornings, he found Saul and his wife, Lisa, sitting at the kitchen table, talking. But unlike most mornings, this time they were talking about pirates.

Instantly, dad's eyes lit up and he blurted out, "I just had the most amazing dream about pirates, and guess what? I invited both of you to join me on a pirate adventure, but neither of you would believe me, so I went by myself."

Mom and Saul looked at each other with wry smiles and then both said, "Really!"

And dad replied, "Really."

When you go to sleep tonight, where will your dreams take you?

- The End -